Samuel French Acting Edition

Important Hats of the Twentieth Century

by Nick Jones

I0591762

‖SAMUEL FRENCH‖

SAMUELFRENCH.COM   SAMUELFRENCH.CO.UK

IMPORTANT HATS OF THE TWENTIETH CENTURY was first produced by the Manhattan Theatre Club; Lynne Meadow, Artistic Director; Barry Grove, Executive Producer, on November 10, 2015. The performance was directed by Mortiz Von Stuelpnagel, with scenic design by Timothy R. Mackabee, lighting design by Jason Lyons, costumes by Jennifer Moeller, original music and sound design by Palmer Hefferan, hair and wig design by Leah J. Loukas, and fight direction by Robert Westley. The Production Stage Manager was Rachel Bauder and the Stage Manager was Betsy Selman. The cast was as follows: Remy Auberjonois, Jon Bass, John Behlmann, Reed Campbell, Carson Elrod, Maria Elena Ramirez, Matthew Saldivar, Triney Sandoval, Henry Vick.

CHARACTERS

SAM GREEVY – early/mid-thirties

T.B. DOYLE – mid-thirties

PAUL ROMS – late twenties/early thirties

DARRYL – man in his early forties

BEV – a woman in her thirties

JONATHAN – a boy of sixteen

KERN – a New York cop, circa 1937

STAN – an Albany cop, circa 1998

BROOKS – an Albany cop, circa 1998

BILLY BARNES – the editor of the *New York Tribune.*

WINSTON DIRK – a radio announcer

JAY GOULD – another radio announcer

A BUTTERFLY – a puppet

There are total roles for eight men, and one woman.

SAM, **DOYLE**, and **PAUL** play single roles. **KERN** doubles as the **FRENCH CORSAIR**. Others plays multiple parts:

JONATHAN / REPORTER 1 / JAY GOULD / ROMAN SOLDIER....	Man 1
DOCTOR CROMWELL / WINSTON DIRK / BROOKS / SHEEP HERDER.....................................	Man 2
DARRYL / BILLY BARNES / MAN IN UNDERSHIRT / MUTANT MONSTER 1 / FIREMAN / TURK IN OTTOMAN EMPIRE.........................	Man 3
JIMMY THE BUTTON MAN / REPORTER 2 / STAN / MUTANT MONSTER 2 / PEDESTRIAN / ABRAHAM LINCOLN	Man 4
NURSE / BEV / MARGARET / SECRETARY / NOBLEWOMAN....	Woman

SETTING

New York City & Albany

TIME

1937 & 1998

AUTHOR'S NOTE

This is a play which is almost but not quite a radio play. I say almost, because as you will see there are many elements which feel like they are straight out of an old noir or sci-fi story from the thirties, including way too many characters, locations, and impossible stage directions. It seems like it should be a radio play, and yet...it is not. Somehow, I expect you to figure out how to stage this. I'm sorry. I think I thought I was writing a radio play but couldn't quite commit. I feel I should mention this, so you won't question whether or not you should employ sound effects and crazy, affected voices. You should. Just try to keep the emotional stakes real in the relationship between Sam Greevy and T.B. Doyle. That will help anchor the rest of the insanity.

Punctuation Note: A "/" indicates overlapping dialogue

ACT I

1.

(New York City, 1937. The street outside the laboratory of **DOCTOR CROMWELL**. *A cop,* **OFFICER KERN**, *is exiting the building. A reporter,* **T.B. DOYLE**, *is waiting for him, notepad in hand.* **DOYLE** *wears some flashy version of a fedora.)*

T.B. DOYLE. Excuse me, Officer Kern. T.B. Doyle, *New York Tribune.*

KERN. *(Looking at his hat.)* Oh!

T.B. DOYLE. Wondering if you could fill me in on /this –

KERN. …I like that hat. Where'd you get that hat?

T.B. DOYLE. My…friend made it for me. So about this crime scene…

KERN. That's chic. Wish I could wear a hat like that.

T.B. DOYLE. Oh, well, I think you could pull it off.

KERN. Nah. Not while I'm a beat cop. Only detectives get to wear their own clothes.

(Sighs.)

T.B. DOYLE. So about this crime…

KERN. Right. What do you want to know?

T.B. DOYLE. *(Scribbling.)* What is it?

KERN. A crime? That's when you break /the –

T.B. DOYLE. What is *this* crime?

KERN. Oh this one here, it's what we call a break in. This is the laboratory of Doctor Cromwell.

T.B. DOYLE. Cromwell? The brilliant overweight scientist?

KERN. Yeah, he's fat. He lost some equipment.

T.B. DOYLE. What kind of equipment?

KERN. A machine, reportedly. Purportedly? What am I trying to say?

T.B. DOYLE. What did the machine *do*?

KERN. The machine. Oh well, what they said was…oh what they said was…oh don't tell me, it…pulses matter at the speed of light – that's it!

T.B. DOYLE. But what does that mean?

KERN. I got no idea. But the doctor sure was cracked up about it. Talking about grave consequences and yadda yadda yadda. But you know these scientists – they think the whole world revolves around science – ha!

T.B. DOYLE. Right.

KERN. Hey maybe next time he can make a machine that will help him lose some weight, eh bub?

T.B. DOYLE. Yeah…

KERN. Ha!

T.B. DOYLE. Say, would it be possible for me to see the doctor?

KERN. Nah, he ain't here. But if you want you can talk to my sergeant. He likes reporters. But that's just cuz he likes to have his picture taken. Me, I get self conscious. Though maybe if I had nicer clothes.

(Sighs.)

T.B. DOYLE. I think I'll try the doctor in his office tomorrow.

(He starts to go.)

KERN. Have it your way, bub. Good luck with your many endeavors.

*(**T.B. DOYLE** stops, turns back.)*

T.B. DOYLE. Hey kid.

(He throws him the hat.)

KERN. You're giving me your hat?

T.B. DOYLE. Go on.

KERN. Thanks, bub.

    (He sees the label.)

Wait! This is a Sam Greevy! That's your friend?

T.B. DOYLE. Heard of him?

KERN. Heard of him? He's the biggest designer in New York!

T.B. DOYLE. Enjoy the hat, kid.

2.

(**SAM GREEVY** *pushes through a crowd of reporters on the street. He is dressed sharply in the current style.*)

REPORTER 1. Mr. Greevy!

REPORTER 2. Mr. Greevy! Couple of words for the paper.

SAM. Not now, gentlemen.

REPORTER 1. But just a few words: Tell us 'bout your newest dress for Julie Bourdain?

REPORTER 2. Will it be red?

REPORTER 1. Will it be blue?

REPORTER 2. Will it be blue-red?

REPORTER 1. That's purple.

REPORTER 2. Will it be purple?

REPORTER 1. Would you consider a green dress, Mr. Greevy? Mr. Greevy!

SAM. Gentlemen, gentlemen, I will do whatever it takes to make women beautiful. Now, if you'll excuse me.

REPORTER 1. Mr. Greevy, wait. Let me touch your trousers.

REPORTER 2. (*Pulling a baby out of his bag.*) Touch my sick child, Mr. Greevy. Mr. Greevy!

(**SAM** *enters a boutique and closes the door behind him. This is the shop of* **PAUL ROMS**. *There are some cutting tables, a sewing machine, and several dress forms with 1990s era sweatshirts on them.* **SAM** *stands by a drafting table.*)

SAM. Oh dear. Those reporters just can't get enough of me. What a nuisance.

PAUL. Excuse me, but we're closed.

SAM. Oh don't worry I'm not here to buy anything. Just paying a little visit. When I heard Paul Roms started his own boutique I just had to see it for myself.

PAUL. (*With epic gravitas.*) Hello Sam.

SAM. (*Same.*) Hello Paul.

Well. It's no George Manuel, but it's no Cornish hen house, either. I'm just glad to see you're still working. I was so upset when you were thrown out of the academy.

PAUL. Of course I'm working. When an idea is born inside me, I can't sleep until I find its perfect form. The academy never learned to accept that. They wanted me to sleep more regularly.

SAM. Oh well no matter, you never needed them in the first place. I'm sorry I've been out of touch but you know I've been ever so busy, and besides, I knew you'd land on your feet. Do you still have that job you had in the college, in the mine?

PAUL. No. That was a summer job.

SAM. Oh yes, a *janitor* – that's what I heard you were doing. Good for you. Important work. We need people to take away our trash, just like we need people to make it. What's this?

(Touching the sweatshirt.)

PAUL. Just something I'm working on. I call it a sweatshirt.

SAM. Mm, that's rich. Is it for a man or a woman?

PAUL. Both.

SAM. Paul, take some advice and leave your crazy ideas on the crazy desk. You're just starting out: you should make some dresses, like the kind a starlet would wear. You know, something flamboyant, with little ball things on it. That's how I got my break. And look at me: five years out of school and already I'm personal designer for Julie Bourdain.

PAUL. Who's Julie Bourdain?

SAM. Who's Julie Bourdain?! Why she's only the biggest singer in New York! Don't you listen to the radio!

PAUL. No. It distracts me.

SAM. You just work here in silence?

PAUL. I enjoy the silence. I enjoyed that about the mine. When you work in a mine you don't have to listen to other's opinions, you get to just toil there in the dark;

and the work is pure, and when work is pure it's more valuable than a diamond.

SAM. Paul I'm sorry to be the one to tell you this but if you're going to make it in this business you probably shouldn't let anyone hear you speak. This is New York. That attitude won't fly here. You've got to keep up on things. The trends. What's happening in Paris. Who's making deals with whom. Who's eating what food made by what chef and in what portions.

PAUL. Why did you come here, Sam?

SAM. Paul. Paul. Paul. Paul. I think you've got talent, Paul. I think you could do something remarkable, if you'd only stop trying to be so modern all the time. I mean look at this thing, it's like a potato sack. You can't treat a woman like a potato, Paul; she needs to feel beautiful. She wants to make an impression. She wants to stand out from the crowd. She wants to wear clothes with zing, with sparkle, with pizzazz, with zap.

PAUL. I don't believe in those words anymore.

SAM. What?

I don't want to make the kind of clothes only celebrities can wear. I want to make practical clothes for regular people.

Regular peop – Okay that's fine; yes obviously they need to wear clothes too, but what about glamour, Paul? What about beauty? You need something for beautiful women to model in department stores – that's plain old horse sense.

PAUL. No. No shows.

SAM. What do you mean, no shows?

PAUL. I don't want people to buy my clothes for the way they look. I want them to buy them for the way they feel. They can try them on right here in the shop. If they like them, they can buy them.

SAM. And if they don't like them?

PAUL. *(Defiantly.)* Then they can't feel.

SAM. Well you're certainly sure of yourself, aren't you?

PAUL. I have respect for my vision.

SAM. Well I think you should get your eyes checked. But alright, have it your way. Don't say I didn't warn you. Oh and Paul how much for the sweatrag or whatever you call it.

PAUL. You want to buy one?

SAM. Oh sure just as a patronizing gesture. I'm just kidding. But seriously, I'm sure you need the money...

> *(He opens his wallet, slaps down a twenty, takes the sweatshirt and leaves.)*

3.

(The apartment of **T.B. DOYLE**, *where* **SAM** *has spent the night.* **SAM** *is eating breakfast while reading the morning paper.)*

SAM. Here it is.

*(***DOYLE** *comes to read over his shoulder.)*

"Sam Greevy's first dress for Julie Bourdain this season was sensational. With light flowing fabrics, bright Eastern prints, and sumptuous dangling ball things, the garment was verging on garish but restrained in all the right places. Though few regular people could pull off such flamboyance, Greevy's talents perfectly match the larger than life ambition of Miss Bourdain, and prove that he is still unquestionably New York's King of Dresses…"

(He takes in this last line, considering it.)

King of Dresses.

T.B. DOYLE. Read on.

SAM. "Julie Bourdain's choice of Sam Greevy as her exclusive designer for the 1937 season has raised its fair share of eyebrows, and inspired speculation as to whether their relationship extends beyond the professional – Oooh! – Ted! Speculation about an affair! That's wonderful!

T.B. DOYLE. I thought it might be nice to start some rumors.

SAM. Rumors, ha! I'll be in the papers for weeks!

(He kisses **T.B. DOYLE**.*)*

So, what was garish?

T.B. DOYLE. Oh Sam…

SAM. Garish is what people want! Big, bold, brassy.

T.B. DOYLE. I know.

SAM. Well then why'd you say it? What was it, the hat? It was the hat, wasn't it?

T.B. DOYLE. The hat was a bit outrageous.

SAM. It had to be! Julie's a radio star not a movie star. If she doesn't have an outrageous hat, how is anyone going to know she's famous?

T.B. DOYLE. Well there's other ways to get attention, besides being so Baroque.

SAM. Oh now I'm Baroque...

T.B. DOYLE. I just love it when you let yourself be more free. I know you have other ideas in you. Bold ideas.

(He holds up the sweatshirt.)

SAM. Where did you get that?

T.B. DOYLE. It was on your sewing table. However did you come up with this, you mad genius?

SAM. Oh that, well that's –

T.B. DOYLE. This is the sort of thing most fashion designers wouldn't touch. Something so forgiving of the body. Why anybody could wear this. It will revolutionize –

SAM. It's not mine.

T.B. DOYLE. And so dreary, yech.

SAM. It was made by someone I knew in the academy. Paul Roms.

T.B. DOYLE. That new designer on Church Street?

SAM. *(Stunned.)* You've heard of him?

T.B. DOYLE. Yeah. But only because he's such a nut ball. Oh I didn't see the back on this, oh this is awful.

SAM. Ted, what are they saying about him? Give it to me straight.

T.B. DOYLE. Some retailers are excited about his understatedness. They think customers are still feeling unsure of themselves after the Depression and want clothing that reflects that.

SAM. Who told you that?

T.B. DOYLE. That's just the word on the street. A homeless man told me.

SAM. Well that's probably why they're homeless. If people wear clothes that set them apart, they'll gain self confidence. What else have you heard?

T.B. DOYLE. Well, I heard he got himself a contract with McCalleister's.

SAM. *What?* Out of nowhere, just like that?! How is that possible?

T.B. DOYLE. *("Search me.")* Maybe he has a family connection.

SAM. Family connection? He's not connected to the earth under his feet. All big ideas and no real talent for fabric construction. He got thrown out of fashion academy for arguing with the professors. He's full of applesauce.

T.B. DOYLE. Then what are you worried about?

SAM. Who said I'm worried?

T.B. DOYLE. Seems like he gets under your skin is all I'm saying.

SAM. Did you really like the new work?

T.B. DOYLE. I gave you a rave.

SAM. You said it was worthy. You didn't even mention the brocade.

T.B. DOYLE. *(Realizing.)* Oh god is that really the time?

(He prepares to leave.)

SAM. What?

T.B. DOYLE. I have to go.

SAM. But I thought we were going to make crepes.

T.B. DOYLE. Put one on ice for me, baby. I have to run down to the Hugely Experimental Science Center for an interview.

SAM. An interview with whom?

T.B. DOYLE. Dr. Cromwell. The brilliant overweight scientist. You know, he's the guy who did all the dirigible research during the war.

SAM. Oh yes, I remember that nut crack. Why do you want to talk to him? You're a fashion reporter.

T.B. DOYLE. Times are tough. They're having me take on some extra assignments. He lost some sort of machine. Doomsday machine by the sound of it.

SAM. Oh these scientists. Why don't they just give up?

4.

(A teenage boy's room, Albany, circa 1998. **JONATHAN**, *sixteen, is moving folded clothes from a laundry basket into his dresser.)*

JONATHAN. *(Calling out.)* Mooommmmmm! Have you seen my blue sweatshirt?

BEV. *(Offstage.)* It should be in your dresser. I remember washing it.

JONATHAN. It's not here!

> *(Softly, sulkily.)*

Don't wash my clothes if you're always going to lose them.

BEV. Why don't you wear that red sweater that Aunt Mary made you?

JONATHAN. Because.

BEV. Because what?

JONATHAN. Because I don't want to get my ass beat, okay?!

> *(Mutters.)*

Stupid…

BEV. You're saying someone's going to give you a hard time because you wear a nice red sweater?

JONATHAN. That's NOT what I said. I said I'd get MY ASS /BEAT

BEV. Language /Jonathan.

JONATHAN. My BUTT. Beat up. Because I wear some lame sweaters my relatives send me. Like I got no style. Why can't you just get me the Sean Jean tracksuits I told you to get??

> *(Behind the closed door of a closet, there is a flash of a light, and a zapping sound. A second later,* **PAUL ROMS** *bursts from the closet. He is wearing a strange metal apparatus on his head. He quickly scans the room, grabs a hat off of* **JONATHAN**'s *desk, and runs back into the closet, closing the door*

behind him. There is a another flash, a zap, and he's gone. **JONATHAN** *stands dumbstruck for a beat, then...)*

JONATHAN. Mommmm!

(...He runs offstage.)

5.

(**DOCTOR CROMWELL** *awakens with a start. There is a knocking on the door.*)

NURSE. Doctor Cromwell? Doctor Cromwell?

CROMWELL. Yes? What is it?

NURSE. There's a reporter to see you.

CROMWELL. Send him away. I have nothing more to say.

NURSE. I tried, Doctor.

T.B. DOYLE. *(Offstage.)* Doctor Cromwell? Don't you think it would be wise to bring this crime to the public notice?

CROMWELL. It's too late. We are doomed.

(**T.B. DOYLE** *pushes his way in.*)

T.B. DOYLE. Well sure eventually, but in the meantime don't you want to see your name in the paper?

NURSE. Sir. You have to leave…

T.B. DOYLE. What if someone knows something and they can help you get your machine back?

NURSE. Sir! I must give the doctor his bath.

CROMWELL. It's alright Fanny. Baths are pointless now.

NURSE. Well, I don't think so.

CROMWELL. Then why don't you take my bath for me?

NURSE. I don't think it works that way.
    (Less confident.) Does it?

(**NURSE** *exits.*)

T.B. DOYLE. Dames, eh? Thanks for your time, Doc.

CROMWELL. You're only wasting your own. I've already told everything to the police.

T.B. DOYLE. Yeah and how's that working for you? The police have their hands full with the big fashion fair coming up. There's not a lot of manpower to chase down machines that nobody understands. So why don't you start by telling me what this whozit-whatzit does that you're so broken up about?

CROMWELL. You wouldn't understand.

T.B. DOYLE. Didn't I just say that. And why are you being so cagey?

CROMWELL. The truth is complicated.

T.B. DOYLE. That doesn't scare me.

CROMWELL. It also can be...embarrassing.

T.B. DOYLE. Do tell.

CROMWELL. What if I told you I had created a machine capable of ending life as we knew it.

T.B. DOYLE. I'd say that sounds like good copy. Are we talking about a weapon?

CROMWELL. Not quite.

T.B. DOYLE. ...Because if you made a weapon that ends life as we know it, that's nothing to be embarrassed about; lots of people would brag about something like that. Or are you afraid of boasting, after what happened with the dirigible industry?

CROMWELL. *(Defensive.)* Don't you start about that. That wasn't my fault/ ...That wasn't my fault...

T.B. DOYLE. *("Easy.")* Alright...

CROMWELL. *(Wistful, then furious.)* I dreamed of a perfect future. Gas powered airships could have ushered in a golden age of air travel: safe, clean, and humongous. But the public didn't understand the science. And the press, all the press wanted to do was crack jokes about my weight.

T.B. DOYLE. Whoa, slow down. Dirigible stocks tanked because of the Hindenberg. And if people compared your body to a blimp that's only human nature, Doc.

CROMWELL. Yes. Human nature. How foolish I was, to think we could rise above the superficial. I couldn't see the future then.

T.B. DOYLE. See the future? Are you feeling alright?

CROMWELL. No. I feel terrible. I've felt terrible for years. And it's your fault, newspaper man!

T.B. DOYLE. Hey now, Doc, that's not fair. I didn't steal your machine.

CROMWELL. No, but if it wasn't for you and your ilk I never would have tried to build it.

T.B. DOYLE. What? Listen, Doc, you're not saying you created a weapon to end life as we know it because people made fun of your weight are you?

CROMWELL. There is nothing wrong with my weight! I just have a round face! Oh what's the point? You press are all the same: rattling on about things you don't understand; passing judgments on people you know nothing about. Well I'm through with you chuckleheads! You're not worthy of my genius.

> *(Intense, mournful.)*

Oh Caroline, why didn't you transduce the molecules the way you were supposed to?

T.B. DOYLE. Wait, who's Caroline? I thought the nurse's name was Fanny.

CROMWELL. Oh just get out! GET OUT!

T.B. DOYLE. Alright, alright. No need to use an outdoor voice, I'm going.

> *(He exits, passing* **NURSE** *as she emerges in a bathrobe.)*

NURSE. Oh! You're done already?

T.B. DOYLE. Nah, this was a trip for biscuits. This ain't the Cromwell I came here for. He's gone loopy as a corkscrew.

CROMWELL. *(Screaming after him.)* Corkscrews! What do you know about corkscrews? I invented the self-cleaning oven! I invented the self-ironing shirt! I created a serum that made cats less selfish. Me! Did you put that in the paper? No! Too busy covering the fashion fairs and world events. Well just you wait, newspaperman! Someday science will have its own section in the paper! And someday, it will be the scientists who are the film and radio stars! It will be the scientists who model clothing in department stores! And that clothing will be like nothing that has ever been seen before!

   (Blackout.)

6.

(Albany. 1998. **DARRYL,** **JONATHAN**'s *father,*
is holding the door open, while **BEV** *sits with*
JONATHAN *on the bed.)*

JONATHAN. I am not crazy. There was a man. He ran out of
the closet, took my hat and disappeared.

BEV. Maybe your hat just fell off and it *felt like* someone was
taking it.

JONATHAN. I wasn't wearing it. And where is it then?

BEV. I don't know, honey, just calm down.

(**DARRYL** *steps forward.*)

DARRYL. Okay, look into my eyes.

BEV. Darryl…

JONATHAN. What? Why?

DARRYL. Are you on drugs? I mean besides pot.

JONATHAN. No no. I don't even smoke pot, I told you.

DARRYL. *(Amused.)* Well we all know that's not true.

BEV. Darryl, this isn't the /time.

JONATHAN. What?? This is such BULLSHIT. There was a
MAN IN MY ROOM!

(Beat.)

DARRYL. Well it just seems…

JONATHAN. WHAT?! /

DARRYL. Strange, it's just strange.

BEV. Darryl. We need to respect that Jonathan saw what he
saw. Just let him finish telling the story.

JONATHAN. Just forget it alright. Just fucking forget it.

DARRYL. We can't forget it. We care about you – wait, did
you just say "fucking"?

BEV. Let's just all listen a /moment.

DARRYL. But he knows…we've told /him…

BEV. Let's listen to Jonathan.

(Beat.)

JONATHAN. Look, if I was on drugs, I would know not to tell my parents that I saw something like this. Okay? But I'm not on drugs so that makes it even more messed up... God, I thought I could trust you...

BEV. Honey, of course you can trust us. Right, Darryl?

DARRYL. Right. We want you to feel like you can trust us of course. I didn't mean to belittle what you saw but / it just –

JONATHAN. I didn't just SEE HIM! He TOOK – MY HAT – OFF MY DESK!

BEV. Jonathan. It's Dad's turn to speak.

DARRYL. I don't want to make you feel like you can't tell us anything. We will look out for this man. And your hat. It was the one with the marijuana leaf on it, right?

JONATHAN. So?

DARRYL. Okay. Now can you do something for us?

JONATHAN. What?

DARRYL. Just so we can eliminate all suspicion.

(He takes out a urine analysis kit, and begins opening it.)

JONATHAN. What?! A piss test? /Are you kidding me?

BEV. Darryl, are you sure?

DARRYL. It would make me feel /better.

JONATHAN. I can't believe this!

DARRYL. Now don't make a big deal about /it.

JONATHAN. This is so... *(To BEV.)* Did you know about this?

DARRYL. It's just urine. What, are you saving it?

JONATHAN. *(Softly.)* So fucking...

DARRYL. What? WHAT? If I hear that word one more time...

JONATHAN. But this is so ffffff –

BEV. *(Warning.)* Jonathan...

JONATHAN. fffffFUCKED! SO FUCKING FUCK /ED!

DARRYL. Grounded! You're grounded.

BEV. Oh Jonathan…why, honey?

DARRYL. We will not be spoken to that /way.

BEV. I know.

DARRYL. I warned you. We warned him. You think I'd have a job if I went around dropping F-bombs all the time? Yeah sure. "Welcome to Sizzler, here's your fucking steak."

(*JONATHAN begins to cry.*)

JONATHAN. I don't care. Just leave me alone.

DARRYL. Alone is all you're going to be, your whole life, using that language.

BEV. Oh Jonathan…

DARRYL. No! Don't rescue him. You think women are going to think you're cool because you use curse words? Wrong. They're not. You better shape up.

(*JONATHAN is really sobbing now, violently.* **DARRYL** *heads to the door.* **BEV** *lingers, pitying her son.*)

JONATHAN. I didn't – I didn't… d-do…anything.

DARRYL. Bev?

BEV. Maybe if he fills up the cup, we can show leniency this once…

DARRYL. Sheila said not to rescue him.

BEV. (*Pleading.*) Darryl?

(*Pause, as* **DARRYL** *mulls it over.*)

DARRYL. Okay. We'll remove the grounding if you fill up the cup with urine.

BEV. How does that sound, Jonathan? Fill the cup with urine?

DARRYL. Hey? Champ? A little bit of urine?

BEV. Jonathan? Will you fill this with urine /for us?

JONATHAN. FINE. YES. Just stop talking about it.

BEV.	DARRYL.
Oh good.	I'll just leave it here.

(He puts the bottle on the desk.)

DARRYL. And I'm sorry if it seemed like I implied that women won't like you, because I know that's not true.

BEV. No, of course they will…

DARRYL. …and actually, I've been thinking we should talk about that stuff, so maybe after you finish filling the cup with urine, we can talk, hey?

JONATHAN. Fine. Just. Fine.

(JONATHAN looks into his father's eyes a moment. DARRYL pats him on the back, then leaves.)

BEV. *(Whispered.)* Thank you, sweetie.

(BEV tries to touch JONATHAN as she leaves, but he shakes her off.)

DARRYL. Mom.

(BEV exits. A few beats, then there is a flash, zap, and once again PAUL ROMS emerges from the closet.)

JONATHAN. DAD! DAD! /MOM!

PAUL. Don't interfere.

JONATHAN. He's back! Come here! Quickly!

(PAUL grabs a tracksuit from JONATHAN, who holds onto it.)

PAUL. Hands off the threads, kid.

JONATHAN. It's mine!

PAUL. *(Holding up his fist.)* You want to hear a little chin music?

(DARRYL enters the room just in time to see him disappear into the closet. Flash. Zap.)

DARRYL. Hey!

JONATHAN. There. There he is. You see it?! Do something.

(DARRYL rushes forward and throws open the door, but PAUL is gone. He closes the door behind him.)

DARRYL. What the fuck!

JONATHAN. You see? You see? I'm not crazy!

(BEV enters.)

BEV. What's going on?

(Flash. Zap. Again, PAUL ROMS comes out of the closet.)

OH! DARRYL!

(PAUL punches JONATHAN in the face and takes something else…)

PAUL. You shoulda listened.

(…Then attempts to return to the closet, but this time DARRYL grabs him. A struggle ensues.)

PAUL ROMS. Please, please no. Please let go…

DARRYL. Who are you? Who are you, and why are you in my son's closet?!

PAUL. Please! Let go…

DARRYL. Are you some kind of pervert, huh?! Huh?!

PAUL. No. Leggo leggo leggo!

(There is a blast of light, followed by a blackout. Lights up and DARRYL and PAUL are gone.)

BEV. DARRYL! /

JONATHAN. DAD!

7.

(A fashion show. **WINSTON DIRK** *is a radio broadcaster, reporting off-site.* **JAY GOULD** *is on the floor.)*

WINSTON DIRK. Well hello to everyone out there in Radioland. This is Winston Dirk. I'm here at Douglas's Department Store for the kick off of New York City's First Annual Fashion Fair where Mr. Sam Greevy is displaying his latest *haute couture.* Now there's a lot of lovely ladies out there, and they're togged to the bricks. I wish you could see them, but you can't cuz this is the radio, so I'm going to try to describe this to you. This model is wearing an elegant yellow strapless dress, or you could call it saffron if you really want to get particular, which I guess everybody does, cuz if you ain't particular then I guess they're just being general and being abstract, and I hate abstract art, don't you, Radioland? I hate abstract art about as much as I love looking at ladies in department stores. Oh yeah. This is just ducky. Here comes another couple of models, Radioland. This first woman has a nice figure, but kind of a big nose, but that's alright, the dress fits her well and it looks good. Alright the second woman is, well, the second woman is a man – nevermind, it's just Sam Greevy taking a turn on the runway himself. Alright and now here come another couple of girls, and they are wearing some remarkable hats. One of the hats looks like a little cake that's sort of stuck on the side of her head. I can't even tell how it's staying in place. It's like a bird house. Like a bird house you might see in France, or a dream. Some place where things are topsy-turvy. The other girl's hat looks like a giant black pancake. I think I did see this in a dream, once. Although in the dream it was worn by a crab with the voice of my father. Glad he's not here. You wouldn't have liked my father, Radioland, he was a real pill. Alright now I'm going to turn this over to Jay Gould on the floor, who's going to have a few words with Mr. Greevy, while I continue to look at these women.

JAY GOULD. Thanks Donald. I am here with Mr. Greevy, and first off, I must say, this is a great collection.

SAM. Thank you.

JAY GOULD. But I think I speak for everyone on the planet, when I say I'm dying to see what Julie Bourdain will be wearing later in the week.

SAM. Well, Jay, you know I can't tell you, because that would ruin the surprise. Rest assured, it will be like nothing that's ever been seen before.

WINSTON DIRK. Certainly nothing that's ever been seen in Radioland, because no one sees anything in Radioland...

JAY GOULD. Yes that's true.

WINSTON DIRK. ...Because Radioland is like a land of the blind.

JAY GOULD. Yes –

WINSTON DIRK. Dark, and cold.

JAY GOULD. And what do you say about Paul Roms' invention of the sweatshirt? Will there be a Greevy sweatshirt anytime in the future?

SAM. Well look, Paul Roms is an old friend of mine...

JAY GOULD. Oh?

SAM. ...yes, and he's a very talented young man, but his views are, well just say, he's been a bit misguided. But he's still young and I do hope he recovers from this, because I think he has a lot to offer.

JAY GOULD. Well I've heard his sweatshirts are selling quite well.

SAM. *(Forced smile.)* Are they?

JAY GOULD. Yes. I hear he's starting a factory.

SAM. Oh, good. Good. I'm so happy for him. That's wonderful to hear...

WINSTON DIRK. *(Still watching the fashion show.)* Jiminy, look at this – pardon my French – but this woman is wearing a big ribbon on her head. It's like her head is a present. That's one present I'd like to open. I mean, not in a violent way.

JAY GOULD. I think we know what you mean, Winston.

WINSTON DIRK. I love women. Do they love me? They love my voice. What do I look like? No one knows. Except me.

SAM. Yes well we all love women, that's what this is about. And you know, to return to your question about Paul Roms, I think the problem is that when a man makes clothes that can be worn by both men and women, well you're not taking into account what women want, which is to *look like a woman.*

JAY GOULD. Well you get to be around a lot of beautiful ladies.

SAM. Ha ha, yes. Good thing I'm married. To my work. And a lady.

JAY GOULD. Of course. So no sweatshirts for you. And what do you think about Paul's other invention – the tracksuit?

SAM. *(Irritated.)* Are we still talking about Paul Roms?

WINSTON DIRK. Oh boy. Look at that dress. I guess those are what you call spaghetti straps.

JAY GOULD. Mr. Greevy –?

WINSTON DIRK. ...or linguini straps? Boccacelli? What am I trying to say?

SAM. *(Recovering.)* I wasn't aware he had another invention.

JAY GOULD. Well then I suppose you can't comment on it.

SAM. No. And, so sorry, but I'd better get back to the models. They might need help getting out of their hats.

JAY GOULD. Thank you so much.

SAM. *(As he storms off.)* No, thank you, Jay. Thank *you.*

WINSTON DIRK. Hey say hi to the girls for me will ya? Tell 'em Winston Dirk is a big fan. Of all of them.

(Waving off some invisible producer.)

No I'm not drunk. Get away from me...

JAY GOULD. Well that's all from Douglas's Department store. We'll have more fashion coverage later in the week.

WINSTON DIRK. So long, Radioland. You miserable place of darkness.

8.

(In **T.B. DOYLE**'s *apartment,* **SAM** *paces about, worked up.)*

SAM. ...This goes beyond taste. This is about human dignity. Fashion is meant to challenge us, to make us strive to have bodies beautiful enough to deserve it. If people start embracing clothes that anyone can wear, they'll stop trying to improve themselves. People will stop going to work. Society will crumble.

T.B. DOYLE. Sam, I think you might be overreacting.

SAM. And I think you might be *underreacting*! You should see the way they swoon for his bally-hallelujah. Paul Roms this, Paul Roms that. You would have thought he found the cure for scarlet fever.

T.B. DOYLE. They're dazzled by his originality, that's all.

SAM. Originality? Oh I see. You *like* his work.

T.B. DOYLE. No, of course not.

SAM. Well then why don't you just jump in the sop bucket too, if you think he's so original.

T.B. DOYLE. No, original in a bad way.

SAM. ...Oh sure sure. Well maybe you'd prefer everyone start wearing tracksuits, if you're going to praise someone like that instead of the person you supposedly CARE ABOUT.

T.B. DOYLE. Sam. You're my favorite artist in the whole world.

SAM. ...Are you sure? Because I don't need to keep coming here! Maybe you'd prefer I go LIVE WITH MY WIFE AND KIDS!

(A beat. **T.B. DOYLE** *proceeds with care.)*

T.B. DOYLE. Sam. He's a flash in the pan.

SAM. All it takes is a spark for the world to catch fire.

T.B. DOYLE. Not on my watch, sugarhead. I got this one in the bag.

SAM. You wrote something?

T.B. DOYLE. It was going to be a surprise.

SAM. What'd you write? I didn't see anything.

T.B. DOYLE. It's coming out this Sunday, in my "Week in Style" column.

SAM. About Roms?

T.B. DOYLE. Oh yeah.

SAM. Are you dismissive?

T.B. DOYLE. Mocking.

SAM. Contemptuous?

T.B. DOYLE. Eviscerating. I tore into him like a starved mad badger in a medieval torture chamber.

SAM. Oh Ted.

T.B. DOYLE. It's a bad review like I haven't written in years. And it's my gift to you, face-doll. All my love for you I poured into that hateful hateful article.

SAM. You are so wonderful.

T.B. DOYLE. I meant every word. I think you are the most important fashion designer New York has seen in years. You belong up there with Gerald T. Donkling and Frankie Del Toro Ricardo.

SAM. I know.

T.B. DOYLE. Paul Roms is going nowhere, unless it's on the night train to frumpyville. His clothes are abysmal. Mundane. Morose...

SAM. Yes.

T.B. DOYLE. Terroristic...

SAM. I love you.

T.B. DOYLE. A mockery of what it means to be human. I couldn't praise his clothes if I tried. If someone put a gun to my head and made me be positive, the most I could possibly say is that they're incredibly comfortable. (*A beat.*) But what does that matter?

9.

(BILLY BARNES, editor of the New York Tribune, looks out the window of his office as his SECRETARY stands by.)

BILLY. Look at that city. Look down there on that street. Thousands of people heading out to work. They don't look up. They just trust that the sky isn't falling; that a man like me doesn't throw his stapler out the window. A stapler thrown from this height, that would kill a man for certain. And yet I never throw my stapler out the window. *(A real question.)* Why? *(The answer.)* Because I am a citizen. And it is part of my contract with society that I don't do things like that. Few do. But when you think of all the windows, and all the staplers in New York, it's rather incredible, isn't it? Don't you agree? Alice?

SECRETARY. Yes, Mr. Barnes.

BILLY. I guess in a way it proves that most people are inherently good.

SECRETARY. Yes. Or else they can't be bothered to buy new staplers.

BILLY. That sounds very cynical. I don't like cynical people working for me, Alice. When people are cynical I wonder if they're even Americans.

SECRETARY. Well, I'm just a secretary.

BILLY. That's true. And we'll need secretaries. There are dark times ahead. I can feel it. Can you feel it, Alice? That feeling in my knee? It acts up when there's a storm coming. But the sky is clear. So it's something else. A mind storm. Or arthritis. In any case, I don't like it. Is Doyle out there?

SECRETARY. Yes, sir.

BILLY. Send him in.

*(She goes and **T.B. DOYLE** enters a moment later.)*

T.B. DOYLE. Mr. Barnes, you wanted to see me?

BILLY. Yeah Ted, I need you to get out there and pound the pavement. I need more men on the news beat.

T.B. DOYLE. Again? Sir, with all due respect, I wasn't hired to do real reporting. I've already got my hands full with the fashion fair.

BILLY. Well then you need to start picking up things with your feet, like a monkey. The people have questions and they need them answered, or at least speculated on with uninformed commentary. There are strange things happening in this city. Reports of strange glowing lights in the sky, that aren't stars. Eerie glowing orbs floating around down by the South Street Seaport, and I need you on the story.

T.B. DOYLE. Orbs you say.

BILLY. That's right I said orbs. I could've just said balls, but I went to college. You can say balls in your article though. I don't want to alienate our readers.

T.B. DOYLE. I'll take a read on the rumble. Is that all?

BILLY. No, actually, it's not. This editorial you wrote on Paul Roms.

T.B. DOYLE. Yeah, what about it?

BILLY. I don't like it. You're too hard on him.

T.B. DOYLE. Well it's an opinion piece.

BILLY. Yeah but your opinion is wrong.

T.B. DOYLE. What do you mean?

BILLY. What do you mean, what do I mean?

T.B. DOYLE. What do you mean, what do I mean, what do I mean?

BILLY. I mean I want you to rewrite the article. I happen to know that some of our advertisers are investing in Paul Roms, in that new factory of his. I don't want you gumming up the works.

T.B. DOYLE. Sir, in ten years at this paper I've never once been asked to compromise my opinion –

BILLY. Well I guess we don't talk enough. What's the big deal? It's just fashion.

T.B. DOYLE. There are principles involved.

BILLY. What principles?

T.B. DOYLE. The traditional tenets of beauty and style.

BILLY. Well word on the street is that beauty is a social construct.

T.B. DOYLE. Who told you that?

BILLY. A homeless man, but he's rarely wrong. And just between you and me – and whoever else you want to tell – I like Roms' clothes. I've been wearing these sweatpants all week.

(Emerging from behind his desk.)

And I think I speak for everyone on the planet when I say, I'm not the only one. I'm tired of making an effort. I got other things to think about. Like glowing orbs. Now get out of my office, and get a wiggle on. We got papers to sell.

10.

(Late night in DOCTOR CROMWELL's place. CROMWELL is sitting in a chair, covered in a blanket, eating fruit salad before the fire. The radio is on.)

(We see JAY GOULD and PROFESSOR CLARK-STEWART on the top of the Empire State Building.)

JAY GOULD. Hello good evening, this is Jay Gould and I'm up here at the top of the Empire State Building with Professor Roger Clark-Stewart, of the New York Science Club. Professor Clark-Stewart, can you tell us what we're doing?

PROFESSOR CLARK-STEWART. Yes, I am setting up a viewing station to monitor orb activity, and try to learn what we can of this strange phenomena.

JAY GOULD. Phenomena, that's a fun word. Phenomena – ooh it's windy up here.

PROFESSOR CLARK-STEWART. Yes, this was originally a docking platform for dirigibles.

JAY GOULD. Yikes.

PROFESSOR CLARK-STEWART. Yeah. Hey Radioland, hope you didn't invest in gas powered airships.

(They chuckle, then:)

JAY GOULD. Well then let's talk more about these orb thingies. What are they?

PROFESSOR CLARK-STEWART. *(Doesn't know.)* Well…um… well…

(Hems on.)

JAY GOULD. *(Throwing a lifeline.)* Are they from space?

PROFESSOR CLARK-STEWART. Is that what you heard? Oh, no, we don't know where they're from or what they are. But we've counted them. At this point we have identified thirty-nine distinct floating objects and we are now in the process of assigning them each cute names selected from a pool of submissions from local school kids.

(Points off.)

For instance, that one there with the spikes, rotating menacingly – that's Cottontail.

JAY GOULD. Have you tried shooting guns at them?

PROFESSOR CLARK-STEWART. Yes, that's the first thing we did.

JAY GOULD. And?

PROFESSOR CLARK-STEWART. They seem to be impervious to gunfire.

JAY GOULD. Uh-oh.

PROFESSOR CLARK-STEWART. Yes, but we don't believe them to be dangerous at this time.

JAY GOULD. Why's that?

PROFESSOR CLARK-STEWART. Because the alternative is too terrifying to contemplate.

(CROMWELL turns off the radio.)

CROMWELL. Fools.

NURSE. Doctor.

CROMWELL. Yes, Fanny?

NURSE. Would you like any more fruit salad?

CROMWELL. No. More fruit salad will not be necessary at this time.

NURSE. Alright then. Let me turn those coals for you then.

(She does so.)

CROMWELL. It's a Friday night. You should be out with your friends.

NURSE. And what about you? It's a Friday night for you, too. You're still a young man, for a middle-aged man, and a man ought to leave the house once in a blue moon. Or at least his chair. Let me switch out your blanket.

CROMWELL. The blanket is fine.

NURSE. But it's dirty and there's a rip in it.

CROMWELL. Those aren't the rips you should be worried about. Go home, Fanny. Go be with your loved ones.

NURSE. *(Sotto.)* What if I already am?

CROMWELL.   NURSE.
What?   Nothing.

NURSE. I'll take the garbage on the way out.

    (She exits.)

CROMWELL. Get home safely. Wait, Fanny!

    (Too late. She is gone. He walks to the window, and looks up at the sky.)

All that work, for what? To see the world ripped apart at the seams. You're the fool, Cromwell. This is your fault. These things are going to kill us all. Unless…

    (He is seized with a thought. He goes to his desk, begins making calculations.)

Divide the integer by the power field…Raise the plasma quotient…It's possible.

    (There is a sound from somewhere within the house.)

Hello, who is there?

    (Someone is there in the shadows.)

Show yourself.

    *(**PAUL ROMS** steps into view, wearing the metal apparatus.)*

PAUL. Hello, Doctor.

CROMWELL. You. I should have known.

PAUL. Shoulda woulda coulda. My momma told me not to dwell on the past. Of course, she didn't have a time hat.

CROMWELL. How did you get in here??

PAUL. I let myself in. You probably couldn't hear me because I'm wearing something called "sneakers." They have padded soles which allow a person to move silently, stealthily. Perfect for basketball players, and assassins.

CROMWELL. You have no idea what you've done. You must return that to me at once.

PAUL. Return it? You're dreaming. This was the best idea I ever thought of, stealing the idea you thought of. I'm only here because I need you to fix it. It only goes to 1998. Very limiting, fashion-wise.

CROMWELL. Fashion-wise?

PAUL. What did you think I was a career janitor? I told you I had a passion for fashion the day you hired me. The hat only goes to 1998. I'm always in this kid's room, I think it's in Albany. Can you jigger the doohickeys to make it go other places?

CROMWELL. You're using the machine to steal clothes??

PAUL. Yeah, I'm using it to get a nose on the competition. But I want a bigger nose. I need to keep introducing products, while there's a good buzz. I'm opening a factory. Things are really going great for me.

(There is a growl from offstage. We see the silhouette of DARRYL.)

More or less.

CROMWELL. What is that?

PAUL. His name is Darryl. He was a man once. Something happened on the trip between here and the future. Something...scientific.

DARRYL. *(Zombie moan.)*

CROMWELL. Paul, you have to stop using the machine.

PAUL. Oh, Darryl's alright. IQ isn't everything. I was a C student. And look at me now.

CROMWELL. Paul listen to me. You have to stop. You're ripping holes in the fabric of time and space.

PAUL. Fabric? What fabric?

CROMWELL. The fabric of time and space.

PAUL. Space fabric?

CROMWELL. The point is: man is not meant to travel in time. That's why I threw away the machine. It's too much power for any man to wield.

PAUL. Hm. I bet you believe in raising taxes, too.

CROMWELL. Surely, you must have noticed things have not been going normally. The weather patterns are irregular, and there are glowing orbs in the sky.

PAUL. I don't listen to the radio.

CROMWELL. Do you look at the sky?

PAUL. I'm a New Yorker. Look, are you going to help me fix the hat?

CROMWELL. It's not a hat! Stop calling it that!

PAUL. Well you put it on your head, don't you?

CROMWELL. Yes.

PAUL. Then it's a hat. A time hat. Now are you going to help me with it, or do I need to convince you, with *innuendo?*

CROMWELL. I will not play party to the destruction of the universe.

PAUL. What if I pay you a consulting fee?

CROMWELL. No.

PAUL. Stock options?

CROMWELL. No.

PAUL. A seat on the board of directors?

CROMWELL. Never!

PAUL. *(Darkening.)* Well, I'm real sorry to hear that, Doctor Cromwell. Cuz I don't know from science, and Darryl don't neither. But Darryl, he's a bona fide subhuman now. And he likes listening to the radio.

> (PAUL *turns up the music as* DARRYL *approaches* CROMWELL, *menacingly.)*

CROMWELL. No... Get back!

> *(They struggle.)*

PAUL. There is nothing frivolous about a man's capacity to dream, Doctor Cromwell. My dream is to be a fashion designer and nothing is going to stand in my way of realizing that dream. So I have no talent. So what? Does that mean I shouldn't be afforded the same opportunities as people who do? No! This is America. And if some people end up wearing sneakers and some people end up like Darryl it's because some people are smart enough to be wearing the time hat when the time hat travels through time!

> (PAUL *takes out a vial of a strange substance and force feeds it to* CROMWELL *as* DARRYL *holds him down, and the lights fade.*)

11.

(Hallway of a luxury apartment building. **T.B. DOYLE** *pounds on an apartment door.* **MARGARET**, **SAM**'s *wife, enters through another door and watches, unnoticed at first.)*

T.B. DOYLE. Sam, please, open the door. I'm sorry. I tried to warn you. They made me change the article Sam. My hands were tied. Oh please don't ignore me. I love you. I'd never do anything to hurt you.

MARGARET. You know, sometimes when nobody answers the door it's because they're not home, not because they're ignoring you.

T.B. DOYLE. Margaret. Hello. Do you –

(The door **T.B. DOYLE** *has been beating on opens, revealing a* **MAN IN HIS UNDERSHIRT**, *who stares at him.)*

Oh. Terribly sorry.

MARGARET. We live over here.

(The man closes the door.)

T.B. DOYLE. Margaret, have you seen Sam? I need to speak to him about the article.

MARGARET. Your fashion column; oh yes, he was very upset about it.

T.B. DOYLE. It in no way reflects my true feelings for him.

MARGARET. And what exactly are your true feelings for my husband?

(A **SMALL CHILD** *comes and wraps herself around her leg, looking up at* **T.B. DOYLE**.*)*

CHILD. Mommy.

T.B. DOYLE. I hold him in the utmost esteem. His work is important for our community.

MARGARET. Yes, and you make it important. I think it must be hard being a critic. Always thinking you're right about everything.

T.B. DOYLE. Well it's the posturing that's key.

MARGARET. I can't begin to pretend to think I'm always right, but like you I love my husband, and I care about his work.

T.B. DOYLE. Margaret, if you think there's anything going on –

MARGARET. Let me finish. I know Sam hates Paul, but I'm glad he's out there, shaking things up. We both know competition drives innovation, and we both know Sam's work has become stale lately. Particularly the hats.

T.B. DOYLE. You know where he is, don't you?

MARGARET. He's down at his shop.

T.B. DOYLE. It's two in the morning.

MAN IN UNDERSHIRT. *(Offstage.)* Oh IS IT?

MARGARET. He wanted to work. Work all night, like he used to, before all the success.

T.B. DOYLE. I never meant to hold him back. I wanted to support him.

MARGARET. Then go to him. You're his muse. He once told me all his hats were inspired by you. That it was your head that he imagined as he toiled over the drafting table.

CHILD. Go to him.

T.B. DOYLE. Alright, child. Alright, I will.

12.

(**SAM GREEVY** *is toiling in his shop. Light of morning crashes through factory windows. The radio emits a hiss of static which abruptly ends as* **WINSTON DIRK** *signs on.* **SAM** *slowly awakens.*)

WINSTON DIRK. "There are those men who seek to see their names inscribed on the walls of history. And there are those who seek to tear the walls down, such that a new wall may be erected, with a simpler, less decorative facade. Such is the case of the designer Paul Roms." These words are taken from this morning's edition of the *New York Tribune.* Unless you've been living under a rock, you've already heard of Paul Roms, the visionary designer taking New York by storm. And if you are under a rock, watch out for slugs and turn up your radio, because Mr. Roms is in the studio today.

SAM. Of course he is...

WINSTON DIRK. Mr. Roms, that's quite a review. How does that feel?

PAUL. It's not anything I wouldn't have expected.

WINSTON DIRK. Oh no? So you were fairly confident your fashion would catch on.

PAUL. Well, you never know what's going to happen when you embark on a daring, revolutionary artistic enterprise...

SAM. Oh come on...

PAUL. ...but I sensed the public was ready for a change, if only someone had the courage to show them the way.

WINSTON DIRK. Ha ha, my, you are confident.

PAUL. *(Sharply.)* Why shouldn't I be?

WINSTON DIRK. *(Humbled.)* No reason. And can you tell us about your latest creation we're looking at right now?

PAUL. Certainly. My latest creation is called skater pants. They don't fit right. They're meant to hang just below the buttocks, and the pant leg is crumpled up near the ankles.

SAM. What??

PAUL. The pockets are oversized, too. They serve no functional purpose except maybe to criminals who are trying to conceal a weapon.

SAM. What is he talking about?

WINSTON DIRK. Mind if I ask why?

SAM. Yes, exactly, why?? Why??

PAUL. Why not? Criminals need fashion, too. Unlike some of the more elitist designers out there, I believe in creating garments for all men, regardless of sex, race, or politics.

WINSTON DIRK. Yes, but, it just seems unconventional.

PAUL. Yeah, so? What did convention ever get you, besides a life of ceaseless mediocrity.

WINSTON DIRK. Wow, it's like you know me.

PAUL. I know people. And I know people are tired, of failing to meet the expectations they set for themselves. Through my collections, I hope to encourage the clothes-wearing public to look for beauty in places they never thought to look.

WINSTON DIRK. Like butt cracks?

SAM. No. Beauty is not subjective! It's not!

PAUL. These pants are beautiful for dramatizing the struggle of remaining clothed.

SAM. Applesauce! Applesauce, I say!

WINSTON DIRK. There you have it, folks. Paul Roms, a modern master. Congratulation, Mr. Roms.

PAUL. Congratulations to you, that you got to meet me.

SAM. You think you can just change the rules of the game, don't you? By coming up with all these incredible ideas! Well I'll show you. You think I'm going to let you throw to the squirrels what it took me this long to build! I'll

show you. I'm the King of Dresses, you crummy crum!
I'M THE KING OF DRESSES! I'M THE LORD OF
LADY'S HATS!

> (**SAM** *throws the radio out the window and stands
> there panting. There is some noise on the street,
> people shouting. He peeks out and then ducks back
> in, worried he may have hurt someone. A moment
> later there is a knock at the door.*)

T.B. DOYLE. Sam? Sam, it's Ted.

SAM. What do *you* want?

T.B. DOYLE. Open the door. We need to talk.

SAM. I have nothing to say to you.

T.B. DOYLE. Sam, please open the door. You don't
understand. My editor made me change the article.

> (**SAM** *opens the door.*)

SAM. Well didn't you fight him??

T.B. DOYLE. I tried. He doesn't care one thin dime what I
think. He just wants to appeal to his advertisers.

SAM. His advertisers? How many stores is he selling at?
Nevermind. I'll beat him. I'll beat him, you know why?
Because I understand women. And women will not live
in a world without beauty. They will not go on without
me.

T.B. DOYLE. Sam what are you doing?

SAM. I'm working, what does it look like. Julie's big show
is today.

T.B. DOYLE. But I thought you turned in the collection.

SAM. I'm still working on the final piece.

> (**T.B. DOYLE** *notices something quite large covered
> with a sheet on the table.*)

T.B. DOYLE. Sam, what is it?

SAM. Why do you care? Going to write a nasty review of it?

T.B. DOYLE. I never wrote a nasty review of your work. I
only didn't write a nasty review about someone else.

SAM. It's the same thing in my book. But it doesn't matter. They want clothes that are modern, just wait until they see *this*.

>   *(He pulls off the sheet, revealing a giant metal hat: as far out a creation as he's ever conceived, and wholly impractical.)*

T.B. DOYLE. Sam, what is that?

SAM. It's a hat. The most important hat of my career.

T.B. DOYLE. It looks heavy.

SAM. Of course it's heavy. I set out to make a hat of substance and that substance is lead.

T.B. DOYLE. But Sam, are you sure it's wearable?

SAM. Of course it's wearable! For a woman of vision and verve, and strong neck muscles.

T.B. DOYLE. But Sam, are you sure? It seems risky.

SAM. Of course I'm sure! You think I'd put my career on the line if I wasn't sure? Metal hats are the future, Ted. Soon everyone will be wearing them.

T.B. DOYLE. How do you know?

SAM. Because I have a window on the future. In my mind. And in my heart. And in the girls I had break into Paul Roms' shop and tell me what he's up to.

T.B. DOYLE. What?

SAM. Oh don't be naive, Ted. Where do you think ideas come from? *Out of thin air?* You think they *just come to people*? No. You go after them. This is a business. Paul Roms is making a giant metal hat, alright? That's how I know it's the future. But surprise! My metal hat is going to hit the market first.

T.B. DOYLE. Sam, you're making a knock off?

SAM. It's not a knock off if it hits the market first. Don't look at me like that. I've worked too hard not to succeed. I have to stay on top, or else he's going to be the one dictating popular style, and then we're all in the bargain bin. This is for us! For all of us. Humanity, I mean.

T.B. DOYLE. Sweetheart. I think you ought to wait. Just to make sure it's safe.

SAM. No time. The show is this afternoon.

T.B. DOYLE. Yes, but –

SAM. But *what*?! Look, I know what I'm doing. I know it's heavy; that's why I'm attaching live birds. To offset the weight. This hat is a masterpiece.

T.B. DOYLE. Yes of course, it's magnificent, it's just –

SAM. W*hat*?

T.B. DOYLE. Nothing. What is this? – This lettering?

SAM. Detail work. Paul Roms had the word Caroline inscribed on the side of his hat.

T.B. DOYLE. Caroline?

SAM. Mine's going to say something like… Mary. That's my daughter's name. That will seem paternal.

T.B. DOYLE. Oh my god. Paul's hat isn't a hat.

SAM. What are you talking about?

T.B. DOYLE. It's a machine. Doctor Cromwell, the brilliant overweight scientist, he mentioned Caroline. He called the machine Caroline!

SAM. Ted, I really don't have time to talk about science things. I've got to finish this hat.

T.B. DOYLE. But Sam listen –

SAM. NO YOU LISTEN. I know what I'm doing and I won't have you presuming you can tell me what to do anymore. I'm the King of Dresses. Who are you, you miserable critic. Why, if you can't understand this it's because you're not an artist.

T.B. DOYLE. *(Stung.)* That's a cold thing to say.

SAM. Well it's true, isn't it? That's why you became a critic, isn't it? Because you didn't have the guts to work out any patterns yourself.

T.B. DOYLE. I'm a critic because I believe in promoting the work of others.

SAM. No guts, and no talent. Well I've tired of listening to you, Ted. It's listening to you that's held me back all these years.

T.B. DOYLE. Held you back? I did everything for you!

SAM. *(Withering.)* Well everything never looked so small. I got no time for you, Ted. There's a new age coming and I sure as heck won't be left behind. Because I'm one of the greats. I belong up there with J. Jon Macaroy, and Dirk Monseur, and Tony Tabblesammer.

T.B. DOYLE. But Sam…

SAM. And if you can't recognize true innovation, and true Art when you see it, then maybe you're not cut out to be a critic either.

T.B. DOYLE. Sam… There comes a point when a hat is not a hat.

SAM. A hat is whatever I say is a hat. But this hat…*(Walking to the door, and opening it.)* is *the door.*

T.B. DOYLE. Alright, buttercheeks, have it your way.

> *(He heads out. **SAM** closes the door and returns to his hat.)*

SAM. If there's one thing I know it's that this hat is brilliant. The Eiffel Tower of hats. Mary. Mary. You're going to change everything.

> *(Lights out.)*

End of Act I

ACT II

13.

(A button emporium in the Fashion District. **OFFICER KERN**, *now a plain-clothes detective, is browsing, when he is approached by* **JIMMY THE BUTTON MAN**.)

JIMMY. Hey there, Kern. Haven't seen you in here in a while.

KERN. Oh yeah, well I haven't needed any buttons. I don't see as much action these days. I'm a detective.

JIMMY. Oh congratulations.

KERN. Yeah. Get to wear my own clothes and everything.

JIMMY. Any word about these glowing orbs?

KERN. Oh yeah what about them?

JIMMY. Has anybody figured out what they are, what they're doing?

KERN. Oh yeah I got no idea. I almost forget they're there. It's amazing how fast you get used to something, isn't it?

JIMMY. Yeah I suppose it is.

KERN. As long as they don't break any laws, or take any jobs, they're fine by me.

JIMMY. I guess. Just thought the police or the military might be concerned, that's all.

KERN. Maybe some guys are. Not in my precinct. Most of the other cops are running security at the fashion fair. Can only worry about so many things at once, you know what I mean.

JIMMY. Yeah, that's true.

> (**T.B. DOYLE** *enters.*)

T.B. DOYLE. Officer Kern.

KERN. *Detective* Kern. Good to see you, bub.

T.B. DOYLE. Thank for coming. Sorry I'm late.

KERN. Aw no trouble. Gave me a chance to see the new buttons and notion and lace. Jimmy here's a friend of mine. We used to run in the same gang in Brooklyn. Now he runs the button emporium.

JIMMY. It's a living.

KERN. So what can I help you with? You got traffic tickets? You need someone to disappear?

T.B. DOYLE. No. It's about that machine, that Cromwell lost.

KERN. Cromwell the fatty?

T.B. DOYLE. Yeah, the brilliant scientist. I can't prove it, but I have a hunch that Paul Roms is somehow behind it.

KERN. Paul Roms? Well, that's a wild hunch alright. What are you thinking?

T.B. DOYLE. If you can help me into his factory, maybe we can turn up something.

KERN. Well technically I'd need a warrant, but I suppose we could charm our way in, with *innuendo*.

> (*He reveals the gun under his jacket.*)

I do owe you a favor.

T.B. DOYLE. Thanks Kern, I appreciate it.

> (*As they leave,* **JIMMY** *gets on the phone.*)

JIMMY. Hey Sal, yeah this is Jimmy down at the Button House. Can you get Paul Roms on the phone? We got a problem.

14.

(The factory of **PAUL ROMS**. *Rows of* **WOMEN** *are at sewing machines, working diligently.* **DARRYL** *is also at a sewing machine.)*

KERN. Shucks, what a well-run factory. This must be one of the best sweatshops in the district. You sure this Roms is up to no good?

T.B. DOYLE. Yeah well I think we ought to keep looking. I know he's involved somehow. And I want to take him down.

(Quieter.)

My relationship depends on it.

KERN. Oh what, you mean if you think people find out he stole a doomsday device, they would stop buying his clothes?

T.B. DOYLE. Don't you?

KERN. Depends on the price point, I guess. They sure are affordable. And I don't know, I don't see nothin' out of the ordinary, 'cept for that man at the sewing machine. Hey what's the matter buddy, don't you know that's women's work? I said hey buddy, didn't you hear my little comment, disparaging your masculinity?

(He waves his hand in front of **DARRYL***'s face.)*

DARRYL. *(Small zombie voice.)* Must sew.

KERN. Hey Doyle, I think something is wrong with these employees.

T.B. DOYLE. You know, Kern, I have to agree.

PAUL. And I also must agree.

*(***PAUL*** enters. He holds a gun.)*

The employees have been fed a serum, developed by Cromwell, to make cats less selfish. On humans it has the effect of complete docility.

KERN. Are you Paul Roms?

PAUL. I am. Now if you'll please turn over your weapon, Detective Kern.

KERN. How do you know my name?

(JIMMY *comes forward.*)

JIMMY. Sorry, Kern.

KERN. Jimmy…

JIMMY. I got a contract to move some serious buttons. I got a family now, and a miniature horse. But just do what he tells you and everything will turn out copacetic.

(JIMMY *takes* KERN*'s gun.*)

T.B. DOYLE. You've made these people into zombies.

PAUL. They don't complain, at least not intelligibly.

DARRYL. *(Moans.)*

PAUL. I like to think they're proud of the work they do here. After all, it's an enterprise destined for success.

T.B. DOYLE. What makes you so sure?

PAUL. Oh, I think you know. You wouldn't be here if you hadn't figured it out.

KERN. Not really. We were just poking around.

PAUL. Oh. Jimmy, cover your ears.

JIMMY. Alright, boss.

(JIMMY *covers his ears.*)

PAUL. I have a time hat.

T.B. DOYLE	KERN.
A what?	Beg your pardon?

PAUL. A time hat. That's how this is all possible.

KERN. What's a time hat?

T.B. DOYLE. It's Cromwell's machine.

PAUL. Yes. Created quite by accident, it seems. Like penicillin, and corn flakes. Cromwell was trying to alter the way matter reflected light, in order to create a slimming effect. But instead of inverting the plasma cloud, it *transduced it.* Or something.

KERN. Of course.

JIMMY. Can I take my hands off my ears yet?

PAUL. No.

T.B. DOYLE. So all these revolutionary clothes are from the future. But that's rotten cheating!

PAUL. Oh really? Cheating? As opposed to what? Sleeping with a critic?

KERN. What?

T.B. DOYLE. Nothing.

PAUL. Oh come now, you didn't think Sam was the only one keeping tabs on his competition. Sam paid girls to break into my shop and take pictures of my machine, and I paid those same girls to tail him home. Those girls are hussies. I paid them in shoes.

T.B. DOYLE. It doesn't matter. You may sell more clothes, but Sam Greevy is the one who will be remembered.

PAUL. Ah yes, I'm sure he will be, but not in the way you might hope.

T.B. DOYLE. What are you talking about?

PAUL. Oh didn't you hear? Jimmy, turn the radio to the fashion fair.

JIMMY. *(Still covering his ears.)* What?

PAUL. Turn the radio on!

JIMMY. Oh.

(He turns the radio on.)

WINSTON DIRK. …Ladies and gentlemen, it's a tragic day at J.C. Penney department store, as one of the great women of our age, a singer, a model, a humanitarian probably; Julie Bourdain, is in the hospital with a broken neck.

T.B. DOYLE. No…

WINSTON DIRK. Jay Gould is at the scene. Jay, are there words to express the feelings at J.C. Penney right now?

JAY GOULD. Yes, well I think that right now there is a collective feeling of anger at the designer Sam Greevy. This hat should never have been allowed to reach the market without tests; it certainly should not have been given to a celebrity; and I think the feeling is that it probably should not have weighed two hundred pounds.

WINSTON DIRK. Yes, that does sound rather heavy. So is the mood in the air that hats have gone too far?

JAY GOULD. That's what the air feels like to me, Winston. This could be a turning point. From elaborate over-fancy clothes to casual comfortable attire.

WINSTON DIRK. Casual and comfortable in the mode of Paul Roms?

JAY GOULD. Precisely.

WINSTON DIRK. I love Paul Roms. This clothing is perfect for us guys on the radio because no one sees what we look like, so who cares.

JAY GOULD. Who cares.

WINSTON DIRK. Who Cares: the new collection from Paul Roms.

T.B. DOYLE. Enough!

(The radio is turned off.)

PAUL. You know, I think I'm really starting to like listening to the radio.

T.B. DOYLE. Oh Sam. Poor Sam. This is your fault. You did this to him.

PAUL. Me? What did I do?

T.B. DOYLE. You drove him to this.

PAUL. We all drive each other, Mr. Doyle. That's what it means to live in a free market society. A lot of people had to break their necks before somebody invented the aeroplane. But it's a small price if a great man learns to fly.

T.B. DOYLE. Great?? What makes you great?? That people like your clothes, that you *didn't even design?*

PAUL. All men create. It takes a genius to see what is marketable.

JIMMY. I guess the real question is what makes great art.

PAUL. *(Ignoring* **JIMMY**.*)* I founded an industry. I create jobs.

T.B. DOYLE. Yeah, for zombies.

PAUL. Eh, we don't call them zombies. This is a judgment-free zone. As long as they meet their quotas. As you can see, I produce results.

T.B. DOYLE. Come a little closer, mug, I'll show you a result.

(**PAUL** *seems amused.*)

PAUL. Oh come now, Mr. Doyle. Why all the tough talk? I'd think you'd appreciate my achievements. Aren't you the same T.B. Doyle who once railed against the tyranny of the cumberbund, and the fussiness of American style?

T.B. DOYLE. I was young then.

PAUL. Yes, and then you grew up, and entered into a co-dependent relationship. Well, you can forget about Greevy. He's finished, but I could use a man like you, who knows fashion, and smells like cinnamon.

T.B. DOYLE. I'd smell like English Kippers if I thought it'd move your knob out of my airspace. You really think, for one second, I'd help you?

PAUL. Well you'd have to start at the bottom of course. But I think you could be quite successful if you'd let yourself be more free, untuck your shirt, let yourself go.

T.B. DOYLE. I'll untuck my shirt in hell.

PAUL. Very well. Darryl, show our guests to the Zoo.

(**DARRYL** *leads them away.*)

15.

(On the streets of New York. **SAM GREEVY** *dials on a pay phone. He is drunk, destroyed. In her home, we see his wife* **MARGARET** *answer the phone.)*

MARGARET. Sam? Sam, is that you?

SAM. Margaret…

MARGARET. Oh Sam. I'm so so sorry.

SAM. The ceiling was too low for the birds to fly. But I thought she could handle it.

MARGARET. Is Julie alright?

SAM. She's a vegetable!

MARGARET. But can she still sing? Maybe if it's only on the radio…

SAM. No. People will know. They won't want to listen anymore. It's too depressing, imagining some vegetable woman, some…potato woman. Ha. Potato woman. Clothes for potato people. Once again Paul, YOU WERE RIGHT!

MARGARET. Sam, where are you?

SAM. Downtown. In the gutter. Fashion Capital of the World!

MARGARET. You don't drink.

SAM. Oh no? Well I guess it must be opposite day cuz I'm three sheets to the wind. Got a crumb in my beard, you know what I'm saying, Margaret? Except I don't have a beard, but I might as well grow one. Might as well just grow hair over every inch of my body and become an animal, cuz that's where we're heading. People wear denim in restaurants, Margaret. Black shoes with brown belts. T-shirts in the theater.

(Ad-lib, picking on a visible audience member's dubious fashion choice.)

Barbarians. They're not outside the gate, they're selling tickets in the lobby, and who am I to say the show is no good. I can't even make a hat that lives forever.

MARGARET. No. You'll come back. Your hat was beautiful. It was just ahead of its time.

SAM. Ahead of its time, behind its time, I can't do this anymore.

MARGARET. Sam, wait, /listen.

SAM. Goodbye Margaret.

MARGARET. No Sam don't hang up!

SAM. Say goodbye to Victor and Jon-Bon for me. And Mary – Jerry! Jerry...

> *(Dropping the receiver.)*

The little one is Jerry...crap...

> *(Sounds of explosions and ray gun sounds offstage.)*

Say, what's happening?

MAN. The death balls are coming!

SAM. Death balls? Since when are we calling them death balls?

MAN. Since they started shooting death rays! The *Tribune* coined the term, right after they set it on fire.

SAM. The *Tribune*...

> *(**SAM** runs back to the phone.)*

MAN. Hey, aren't you Sam Greevy?

SAM. *(Ignoring the man.)* Hello, Operator? Operator, connect me to T.B. Doyle.

> *(A **FIREMAN** approaches.)*

FIREMAN. You better get a wiggle on, buddy.

SAM. *(On phone, urgently.)* Hold on. Patricia? Patricia, it's Sam. Can I speak to Ted please?

FIREMAN. Buddy...

SAM. *(On phone.)* What? Where?

FIREMAN. ...You don't have time for this phone call.

SAM. *(On phone, in disbelief)* ...He said he's going *where*?

FIREMAN. Buddy you gotta go.

SAM. To *his factory?*

FIREMAN. You gotta go NOW!

> *(There is a tremendous boom. They turn and look up as a strange orb sound gets louder, and a bright light pours down on them. The* **FIREMAN** *runs away as* **SAM** *stares up into the light, which becomes intensely bright.)*

SAM. Fireman? Fireman! I need assistance!

> *(The sound reaches a screeching pitch.)*
>
> *(Blackout.)*

16.

(PAUL *leads* T.B. DOYLE *and* KERN *into a sub-basement underworld.*)

PAUL. Come right this way. Mind your step. The employees tend to defecate right on the floor.

T.B. DOYLE. What is this place?

PAUL. I don't like paying for electricity, so I created my own power station. The workers' pedalling makes me entirely self-sufficient as well as environmental. Isn't that right, Doctor Cromwell?

(DOCTOR CROMWELL *enters, wearing a beer-drinking hat containing cat serum. He has lost a lot of weight.*)

T.B. DOYLE. Doctor Cromwell? Him?

PAUL. Oh yes. When he refused to help me improve the time hat, I fed him his own cat control serum. He is one of my best workers.

T.B. DOYLE. This is one of our greatest scientific minds.

KERN. He looks great.

PAUL. So will you, after a few fourteen hour days with limited rations.

T.B. DOYLE. Roms, this has gone too far. This is kidnapping. It's wrong.

PAUL. Is it??

T.B. DOYLE. Yes.

PAUL. (*After a beat.*) Touché. But…c'est la vie… Ou et la bibliothèque. That's all the French I know. Bottoms up, gentlemen.

(PAUL *approaches* KERN, *serum in hand, as* DARRYL *holds him down.*)

KERN. Time to join the work force.

(*There are death ray sounds and explosions outside.*)

What is that?

PAUL. I don't know. Jimmy, what's going on out there?

JIMMY. It's the orbs. They're killing people.

PAUL. What? But, now?

JIMMY. Aw nuts, I knew they weren't just for decoration. Maybe you better shut down operations for the day.

PAUL. No! I have orders to fill. Lock the doors, then check the insurance. You two, get in the cage.

KERN. Wait, you can't keep us in here. What if there's a fire?

PAUL. There won't be a fire.

T.B. DOYLE. How can you be sure?

PAUL. There won't be a fire! There can't be. That would be horrible.

(*More explosions upstairs as* PAUL *runs off.*)

Don't let them get away.

(*Then: another major explosion, and a wall collapses. Smoke is beginning to fill the room.*)

KERN. Oh no. Oh no. Damn it, buddy, you've got to let us out. You want some slop, boy? Just let us out, buddy. I'll give you all you want.

T.B. DOYLE. I don't think he's interested in that.

KERN. Well it's all I have to offer!

T.B. DOYLE. Wait, let me talk to him. Darryl, please, you're better than this.

KERN. Do you know him?

T.B. DOYLE. Quiet. Darryl, hey buddy boy, you're not a monster. Sure, you might be brain damaged but deep down I know, you're…not brain damaged. You're good.

(**DARRYL** *looks conflicted, looks at himself, maybe moans a little.*)

Don't look at your clothes, look into your heart.

(**DARRYL**, *confused, looks inside his shirt.*)

No, don't, actually try to…

KERN. That's confusing him, it's too abstract. Wait a minute. Darryl buddy, I know what you need.

(He hands him the Greevy hat he's been wearing.)

Go on, take it. You'll look great in it, I promise.

(DARRYL *puts on the hat.)*

T.B DOYLE.	**KERN**.
Ohhhhh.	Wowww.

KERN. Wow you look great. And looking good is feeling good, right buddy? And feeling good is doing good?

(Another explosion.)

T.B. DOYLE. Help us out, Darryl, please. We know you have goodness inside you.

KERN. And even if you don't, it's all how you carry yourself.

(DARRYL *hesitates, then opens the cage.)*

T.B. DOYLE. Yes Darryl. That's it. Atta boy, Darryl.

KERN. Alright, dust it.

T.B. DOYLE. What about the doctor?

KERN. No time. Come on!

T.B. DOYLE. We can't leave without the doctor, he's the only one who can help turn things normal again.

KERN. *(Irritated.)* Alright, alright, but hurry.

(They help **CROMWELL** *to his feet and get out of there.)*

17.

WINSTON DIRK. Well Radioland, you're not going to believe this, but we're under attack. Who's attacking us? Death balls. That's right I said death balls. Death balls from the sky and they mean business. The streets are on fire. People are running for their lives, dogs are barking and barking and barking and barking. So I think it's safe to say that our fashion fair coverage is going to be somewhat compromised as we deal with these new developments. Jay, are you still there?

(The sound of screaming and pandemonium.)

JAY GOULD. *(Zttt crackle.)* Oh no! *(Crackle crackle static.)*

WINSTON DIRK. Jay? …Jay… Oh god.

(Suddenly, **JAY GOULD** *breaks in.)*

JAY GOULD. No, I'm here. I'm here.

WINSTON DIRK. Oh God Jay, for a moment there I thought you were gone.

JAY GOULD. Well, I did run away. But I'm back now Winston, because, well, I just think it's important that we're here to give people comfort in these dark hours – OH GOD THAT MAN'S HEAD JUST EXPLODED! IT JUST EXPLODED RIGHT IN FRONT OF ME! But I won't run away. If we give into fear, that means the balls have won.

WINSTON DIRK. That's right.

JAY GOULD. We have to just go about our business.

WINSTON DIRK. That's right. So… Who's the hottest designer right now?

JAY GOULD. Hot as in popular, or hot as in on fire? Coco Chanel is dead, her shop in flames, like everything.

WINSTON DIRK. Well where is the fire department in a time like this?

JAY GOULD. Probably in traffic, trying to flee the city, like most people. I saw what it looked like, and figured it was hopeless. That's why I came back to work.

WINSTON DIRK. A noble fatalism, my friend.

JAY GOULD. Thank you, Winston. It's been an honor to work with you.

WINSTON DIRK. Yes. I wish I had time to meet you face to face. Are you a tall man?

JAY GOULD. Not particularly.

WINSTON DIRK. I always imagined you as being tall, and blonde, and leggy.

JAY GOULD. That's not me.

WINSTON DIRK. Well, it doesn't matter now. It kind of makes you wonder.

JAY GOULD. What?

WINSTON DIRK. How many people could be saved, if only we had more dirigibles.

18.

(KERN and T.B. DOYLE try to escape the smoke-filled factory, trying a locked door.)

KERN. It's no use, it's locked. Jimmy, let us out!

JIMMY. Sorry, Kern. I got my orders. You and the girls ain't going nowhere.

KERN. But we're going to burn up in here!

JIMMY. Sorry, Kern. Orders is orders.

KERN. You dirty rat, Jimmy. Running down the street like a coward. I hope you die in that outfit.

(Zap! Outside, a death ray incinerates JIMMY.)

Oh. He did.

CROMWELL. So will all of them who wear the clothing of Paul Roms.

T.B. DOYLE. Doc, you got your voice back.

CROMWELL. Yes, not that anyone listens to me. I told Roms there would be consequences for time-meddling.

(He walks to where the time hat has been left on display.)

T.B. DOYLE. Is that her? Is that Caroline?

CROMWELL. Yes. I named her after my niece. They both started out so full of potential.

Then, at fourteen, Caroline cashed in her middle class life for a ride on the rails and a few sips of dandelion wine. They say America doesn't have a hobo problem, but I'll tell you –

KERN. I'd love to hear the story. Once we get out of here.

CROMWELL. And go where? Time is unraveling. No place is safe.

T.B. DOYLE. Wait. You're saying it's because of your machine that these balls are attacking the city?

CROMWELL. No. The orbs are here to repair the damage. I believe they are part of some regulatory mechanism in time-space. They've come to destroy those facts of history which will not align with the future.

T.B. DOYLE. Like Paul Roms' clothes.

CROMWELL. His clothes, his influence, perhaps this whole swath of time-space, they're going to trim it all off, to restore balance to the universe.

T.B. DOYLE. Like cosmic tailors.

CROMWELL. Indeed.

> (*The door is knocked down, and we behold* **SAM**, *looking heroic with a fireman's axe and helmet.*)

SAM. Ted!

T.B. DOYLE. Sam.

KERN. Oh boy, you're a sight for sore eyes.

SAM. Ted, I don't know why you're here, and I don't care. I couldn't live with myself if I didn't tell you: I made a mistake. I never should have let my career get between us.

KERN. Wait, are you not an actual fireman?

SAM. No, it's just a motif. The real firemen are outside. Everything is in flames.

KERN. Oh well. I guess it doesn't matter. We're all gonna be trimmed off, the doctor says.

SAM. What?

T.B. DOYLE. Sam, something terrible has happened. The world is ending.

SAM. It's Paul's fault, isn't it?

T.B. DOYLE. Yes.

SAM. I knew it. I knew his fashion had consequences.

T.B. DOYLE. You were right.

CROMWELL. Wait. There may be a way. If I can go back in time and stop myself from ever hiring Roms as my janitor, I may be able to repair the casual paradox.

SAM. Casual what?

CROMWELL. The mismatch in the fabric of time and space. I just need to adjust the plasma field.

(CROMWELL *takes the hat and begins to tinker with it, opening a panel, which reveals a dial.*)

T.B. DOYLE. Roms was moving merchandise from the future. That's how he got the jump on you.

SAM. That snake. Cheating with science.

KERN. (*To* CROMWELL.) I see. So when you say the fabric is mismatched, you mean like the way plaid doesn't go with paisley.

CROMWELL. I suppose so.

KERN. Or fur and chiffon.

CROMWELL. I'm actually trying to concentrate.

(*Suddenly,* CROMWELL *finds a gun to his temple.* PAUL *has slipped in undetected.*)

PAUL. Fur and chiffon can work.

T.B. DOYLE. No…

PAUL. Yes. With an accessory to tie it all together.

SAM. You're out of your goddamned mind!

(T.B. DOYLE *holds* SAM *back, as* PAUL *takes the hat from* CROMWELL *and steps back.*)

CROMWELL. No. Give that to me. You're only going to make things worse.

PAUL. Beauty is in the eye of the beholder. It's only because you're so old-fashioned that you can't comprehend the beauty of 1998.

CROMWELL. I'm not talking about fashion.

PAUL. Neither am I. I'm talking profits. Now if you'll excuse me, there's something called a camo tank top, and I already know it will sell.

(PAUL *begins to put on the hat.* SAM *rushes him.*)

SAM. No!

T.B. DOYLE. Sam!

(SAM *crashes into* PAUL *as the time hat activates. They disappear in a flash of light.*)

T.B. DOYLE. Doc. Where are they? 1998.

CROMWELL. Perhaps, had he used the machine properly. He put it on backwards.

T.B. DOYLE. So they're in…

CROMWELL. 8991.

> *(Blackout.)*

19.

(The Year 8991. Wind howls across a barren plain.)

(The men lay disoriented on the ground, near the time hat, which has been thrown some distance away.)

SAM. What is this barren hellscape? This must be 1998. Of course this is where your clothes would come from.

PAUL. No. We're somewhere else. This is wrong. Where is the hat?

(He looks for the hat, and notices for the first time two MUTANT MONSTERS examining it where it has been thrown some distance away.)

(The MONSTERS are completely covered in hair, like sasquatches.)

No... No...

(He comes forward, but one of the MONSTERS threatens him.)

(The MONSTER turns the hat over, trying to figure it out, pulling at wires.)

Don't touch that. It's delicate. Delicate.

(The MONSTER with the hat consults with the other in a foreign tongue. Through their body language, Sam and Paul are able to infer that the monsters think the hat is some sort of sexual device, to put one's genitalia in.)

PAUL.	SAM.
No. No, that's wrong.	No, don't do that. That's not a good idea.

(The MONSTER is preparing to fuck the hat.)

PAUL. No no no no, don't.

>*(He comes forward toward the* MONSTER, *and is held back by the other.)*

No no no no no!

>*(The* MONSTER *drifts offstage while placing his genitalia into the hat. There is a flash of light.)*

>*(Blackout.)*

20.

(1998. JONATHAN's room. The room has been completely torn apart, ransacked, gutted. BROOKS and STAN, two policemen, are shown into the room by JONATHAN and BEV, who look haggard for lack of sleep.)

(Without any other articles of clothing left, JONATHAN is wearing the lame red sweater his grandma gave him.)

BEV. This is where he comes from.

STAN. Here?

BEV. Yes. From the closet.

JONATHAN. I tried to board the door shut, but he keeps busting it open.

BROOKS. I see.

BEV. We already told everything to the other police.

JONATHAN. Yeah like a thousand fucking times.

BEV. Jonathan.

JONATHAN. What?

BEV. Nothing.

(BEV lights up a cigarette.)

BROOKS. Well look, ma'am, we're doing everything we possibly can, but maybe you should…maybe it's not a good idea for you to stay in this house.

JONATHAN. But this is where he comes from. You need to wait here. You need to post a policeman to guard this closet.

STAN. That's not possible.

JONATHAN. Why not?

STAN. It's just not.

JONATHAN. You think we're crazy, don't you?

BROOKS. No, son, it's just –

JONATHAN. Its just you'd rather just drive around aimlessly, looking in the wrong place.

STAN. Listen –

JONATHAN. Or maybe you just don't feel like doing your job.

BEV. Jonathan!

JONATHAN. What?

BEV. I'm sorry. Jonathan, now I'm sure the police are looking into every possible lead. It's just a very difficult situation.

BROOKS. Yes son, we are doing /absolutely...

JONATHAN. And I'm not your son. Unless you're my dad. And I hope you're not. Because you suck.

BROOKS. Maybe we should go.

STAN. Yep.

BROOKS. We'll let you know if we hear anything. Just let us know if you need anything else, besides solving the mystery of your husband's disappearance.

BEV. Well we could use some clothes.

BROOKS. We'll bring some by.

BEV. Thank you.

STAN. We'll be in touch.

   (They exit.)

JONATHAN. Yeah, sure they will. In touch with their dicks. What a bunch of useless idiots.

BEV. Jonathan! Please. Don't talk to the police that way. It will just make things worse.

   (Unnoticed, the **MONSTER** *emerges from the closet, confused.)*

JONATHAN. Okay, sure, worse. Worse than *what? This?*

BEV. It can always get worse. That's something you're too young to understand.

JONATHAN. Well I'm sorry but I'm not willing to just kiss people's asses. Why don't you back me up once in a while?

BEV. I do back you up. I'm on your side.

JONATHAN. *(Emotional.)* Well it doesn't feel like that. It feels like – it feels like…

> (**BEV** *notices the* **MONSTER**.)

BEV. Oh! Jonathan!

> (**BEV** *begins throwing things at the* **MONSTER** *as* **JONATHAN** *scrambles up from the ground. They both start shouting.*)

JONATHAN. Ahhhh!

> *(The* **MONSTER** *throws the hat down on the stripped mattress of* **JONATHAN**'s *bed and goes back in the closet, where he cowers.)*

(Indicating the hat.) Mom.

> *(They understand each other.)*

BEV. That's how he does it.

> (**JONATHAN** *goes for the hat.*)

Wait. Be careful.

JONATHAN. I got it.

> (**JONATHAN** *approaches the hat slowly but then slips and falls. He hits the mattress, and the hat bounces off the bed. There is a flash of light.*)

Oh no.

BEV. OH GOD FUCKING DAMMIT JONATHAN!

> *(Blackout.)*

21.

(The time hat appears in the middle of the forest. The audience is left to just watch the hat for maybe ten seconds, while taking in the sounds of the forest.)

(Eventually, a **BUTTERFLY** *enters and flies around the hat for about twenty seconds, nearly landing on it, but then fluttering away – teasingly.)*

(Finally it lands. A flash of light.)

(Blackout.)

22.

*(8991. A **MONSTER** is lying on the ground, dead. **PAUL** and **SAM** are no longer fighting, but sitting on the ground, hopeless, out of ideas.)*

*(The **BUTTERFLY** and the time hat appear, unnoticed at first. The **BUTTERFLY** flutters around **PAUL** and **SAM**. They follow it with their eyes, until they see the hat. They jump to their feet.)*

*(**SAM** and **PAUL** grab the time hat. They transport again.)*

23.
TIME TRAVEL MONTAGE

*(A **TURK** is seen eating grapes as **PAUL** and **SAM** appear. **PAUL** sees the exposed dial on the time hat and realizes now how he can use it.)*

[Turk In The Ottoman Empire]

PAUL. I get it. These numbers by the dial represent years. Fantastic! I can go anywhere now.

*(**SAM** snatches the hat from him.)*

Sam, what are you doing?

SAM. You're destroying the world.

PAUL. That's just a theory.

(They grapple again. They transport again.)

[Biblical Age Sheep Herder]

*(A **SHEEP HERDER** tends his flock as they continue to fight.)*

PAUL. Stop! You're going to break it.

SAM. Better I break it than live in the world you make.

PAUL. Would you rather live here?

*(The **SHEEP HERDER** bows down.)*

SAM. No.

(Considering.)

Well. No.

(They transport again.)

[Cavalier In A Sword Fight]

*(A **CAVALIER** is in the midst of a sword fight, with an unseen opponent offstage.)*

PAUL. At least I make garments for the masses. You make clothes nobody can wear.

SAM. I make clothes for God to wear.

PAUL. There is no God. And if there is, he's wearing sweatpants.

> (*The* CAVALIER *notices* SAM *and* PAUL *and while distracted gets stabbed in the stomach.*)

> (SAM *and* PAUL *grab the time hat. They transport again.*)

[Lincoln At The Ford Theater]

SAM. I thought you were a genius. You don't believe in anything.

PAUL. Hypocrite. You –

> (*A toilet flushes.* LINCOLN *exits the bathroom.*)

LINCOLN. Don't go in there, boys.

> (*He crosses the stage.*)

> (SAM *and* PAUL *grab the time hat. They transport again.*)

[Soldier In Ancient Rome]

ROMAN SOLDIER. I'm a Roman soldier.

> (PAUL *shoots him.*)

SAM. You're a sociopath.

PAUL. I'm a businessman. Maybe if you learned the first thing about business you could move more than forty units a quarter.

> (*They transport again.*)

[Noblewoman In France]

> (*A* NOBLEWOMAN *is caught unaware in her boudoir.*)

PAUL. Here? Is this what you want? Corsettes and crinoline? Frill and lace?

SAM. There's nothing wrong with elegance, Paul. She's beautiful. You look beautiful.

PAUL. She can't fit through the door.

SAM. It's worth it. If she inspires people. They can come to her room to see her. It's not about her, it's not about me. It's about making something timeless. You'll never make anything rare and fine.

(*Taking the* NOBLEWOMAN*'s hat.*)

God I love this, are these ostrich feathers…?

PAUL. Don't you get it, Sam. I don't need to make anything rare and fine. That's why I win.

(PAUL *has the hat, which he activates.* SAM *jumps on him and together, they tumble through time and space.*)

(*Falling through time:*)

What are you doing, Sam? Beauty is a shell game. Nothing is timeless, because nothing is built to last. You're a fashion designer. You ought to know that.

(*They land in* JONATHAN*'s bedroom.*)

24.

(1998. The **MONSTER** *has been restrained.* **JONATHAN** *is waiting outside the closet with a golf club.)*

*(**PAUL** and **SAM** burst out of the closet and **JONATHAN** hits **SAM** in the face with the golf club.)*

JONATHAN. Mom! Get them!

*(**BEV** charges, and jumps on **PAUL**'s back, as **SAM** falls to the ground holding his head.)*

PAUL. Careful careful, watch the hat.

JONATHAN. Give it to me.

PAUL. Now hold on…

JONATHAN. I said give it to me, motherfucker!

*(**JONATHAN** holds up the golf club.)*

PAUL. Goodness. Now wait.

JONATHAN. I will smash your head you dumb asshole. Take off the hat.

PAUL. Alright. Alright.

*(He takes off the hat. **BEV** gets the gun.)*

What do you want?

SAM. I think you broke my nose…

BEV. WHAT DO WE WANT? WHAT DO WE WANT? We want Darryl, you candy ass sonsofbitches!

JONATHAN. Mom.

BEV. What?

JONATHAN. Nothing. Cool.

BEV. Where is Darryl?

PAUL. Darryl, ah yes, he's great. He's excellent. And doing good work.

SAM. Don't listen to that phony. It's applesauce. It's all applesauce.

PAUL. No, it's not applesauce, it's the truth! You can trust me. Look how I'm dressed. I'm one of you: a future man.

JONATHAN. Shoot them.

>*(BEV comes forward with the gun.)*

PAUL.	SAM.
No, don't.	No, we're not together.

BEV. Oh no? You want to live?

PAUL. Yes.

BEV. Then start talking. What are you doing here? Where did you come from? And what...the fuck...is THAT?

>*(She points to the MONSTER, who is cowering in the corner, fumbling with the French hat, trying to fuck his way back home.)*

PAUL. That...is your husband.

BEV. What?

PAUL. Yes, I was about to say he's been through a lot, but with a shower and a shave, he'll be...right as rain.

>*(As the MONSTER continues to fuck the hat.)*

Maybe get that hat away from him.

SAM. *(Sweet, pitying.)* Oh, he's trying to go home.

>*(As JONATHAN and BEV consider the MONSTER, PAUL goes for the hat.)*

BEV. Jonathan, look out.

>*(BEV shoots at PAUL, blowing out a lightbulb. Blackout. In the darkness, another shot rings out.)*

Where did he go?

>*(She shoots again.)*

JONATHAN. Mom! Don't shoot guns in the dark!

>*(She shoots several more times.)*

MOM!

BEV. But where is he?

JONATHAN. I don't know. I can't hear his footsteps.

> *(Beat.)*

PAUL. *(Whispers.)* Because I'm wearing sneakers.

> *(**BEV** shoots twice. We hear the sound of the time hat powering up.)*

SAM. Wait Paul, don't leave me here. Please Paul. Please… no…

> *(There is a flash of light. **JONATHAN** turns on the light switch.)*

> *(**PAUL** is on the floor, wearing the French hat on his head. **SAM** is gone.)*

PAUL. Oh no. No. NOOOOOOO!

25.

*(*JAY GOULD *reports from the floor of Madison Square Garden, where a great celebration is underway.* WINSTON DIRK *reports from the mezzanine. They face forward toward the audience.)*

WINSTON DIRK. They came from space, and were named by school children. Cottontail. Kooshy-Bush. Arnold the Metal Meatball. Names which shall live in infamy. But as quickly as the balls came, so quickly did they disperse, leaving New York to count our dead, and honor our heroes. Which is why we are gathered here tonight at Madison Square Garden to celebrate the heroes of Ball Day: the policemen, the firemen, the medics, the milliners, all those brave New Yorkers who put their lives on the line to help their fellow man. Jay, what's the scene like on the floor?

JAY GOULD. Well, Winston, it's a veritable who's who of anyone who's anyone, and some who aren't. Everyone's dressed to the nines, and looking sharp.

WINSTON DIRK. I'll bet, with Sam Greevy dressing the honorees.

JAY GOULD. That's right.

WINSTON DIRK. I wish I could be there with you, but they got me up on the mezzanine with the drips. Hey look.

(Waves.)

JAY GOULD. Uh.

WINSTON DIRK. See me?

JAY GOULD. Yes, Winston. I see you.

WINSTON DIRK. Feels good to be seen. And a nice view from up here. Check out the hoots on the bing-bong to your left.

JAY GOULD. *(Looking around.)* Oh is that Sam Greevy? Yes, Sam Greevy's entering the hall...

(He joins other reporters swarming **SAM***, who enters wearing a beautiful suit.)*

JAY GOULD. *(Cont.)* Mr. Greevy, how does it feel to be made New York's first Fashion Commissioner?

SAM. It's an honor.

REPORTER 2. Is it true you're making improvements to the firemen's uniforms, and will they be practical?

SAM. If by practical, you mean stunningly beautiful, then yes, they will be as practical as they come.

*(***REPORTERS*** laugh.)*

I believe all our civil servants deserve to look good. That goes for you boys in the press corp, too.

(They laugh again, harder.)

JAY GOULD. That's rich. Just don't give us any hats made of lead.

(He laughs. Nobody else does. An awkward beat.)

REPORTER 2. Hey is that Julie Bourdain?

JAY GOULD. Julie? A word for the paper, /Julie!

REPORTER. Julie! Wonderful wheelchair…

*(The ***REPORTERS*** run off, cameras flashing. **T.B. DOYLE** approaches.)*

T.B. DOYLE. Mr. Greevy, you're back on top. Why the long face?

SAM. I was just thinking of all the times I'll have to do this.

T.B. DOYLE. Do what?

SAM. Make pretty things, for people I barely know, who wear them once and then wonder what's next? It's fun to go to the circus, it's quite another to live in one. And what's it all for? So I can be famous? So I can be somebody people remember, like George Bankley, or Tyra Sumelle, or Henry T. Blong?

T.B. DOYLE. No. Because you help people.

SAM. Do I?

T.B. DOYLE. Sam, look over there.

(He points to where **KERN**, **CROMWELL**, *and* **DARRYL** *are gathered by a refreshment table, all looking sharp.* **CROMWELL** *is fat again.* **FANNY THE NURSE** *stands by his side.)*

You see how strong and confident those folks look.

KERN. Say Cromwell, did you lose some weight?

CROMWELL. No. I gained some, actually. But I'm wearing vertical stripes.

T.B. DOYLE. You did that for them.

DARRYL. *(Subhuman attempt to join conversation.)*

CROMWELL. Yes, Darryl, we still like your hat.

NURSE. *(Sotto.)* Can't you help him get home?

CROMWELL. *(Sotto.)* No.

SAM. But Cromwell gained all his weight back, and Kern is still a terrible policeman, and Darryl is still brain damaged.

T.B. DOYLE. But they don't *feel that way.*

SAM. I guess so. But the nineties are coming. We're swimming against the tide.

T.B. DOYLE. It doesn't matter.

SAM. Doesn't matter?

T.B. DOYLE. There will always be those who push the limits of good taste. But for every schlub who wears sportswear to Christmas dinner, for every girl in a sexy cat Halloween costume two days past Halloween, for ever man or woman who wears _ to the theater *(Callback to whatever the previously called out audience member is wearing.)* there will be one more who says, "No, I will not dress that way. Because I believe clothes are not just there to cover up my bits and pieces, they *are* my bits, and my pieces, and I want them to look good." That's what we're fighting for. And why we need you.

SAM. You really know how to lay it on thick, don't you, Ted? What's the matter, need a new hat?

(They come together, sweetly.)

T.B. DOYLE. You make it, I'll wear it.

(He smiles.)

Just don't expect me to take care of any damn birds.

(They kiss. Lights fade.)

End of Play